Cuddle Time

Libby Gleeson   illustrated by Julie Vivas

For Charlotte   ~ J.V.

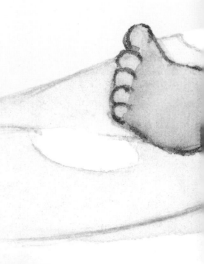

Text copyright © 2004 by Libby Gleeson
Illustrations copyright © 2004 by Julie Vivas

First U.S. edition 2004

Library of Congress Cataloging-in-Publication Data is available.

Library of Congress Catalog Card Number 2003069622

ISBN 0-7636-2320-2

2 4 6 8 10 9 7 5 3 1

Printed in Singapore

This book was typeset in Myriad Tilt.
The illustrations were done in watercolor and pencil.

Candlewick Press
2067 Massachusetts Avenue
Cambridge, Massachusetts 02140

visit us at www.candlewick.com

CANDLEWICK PRESS
CAMBRIDGE, MASSACHUSETTS

The sun slips into our
quiet room.

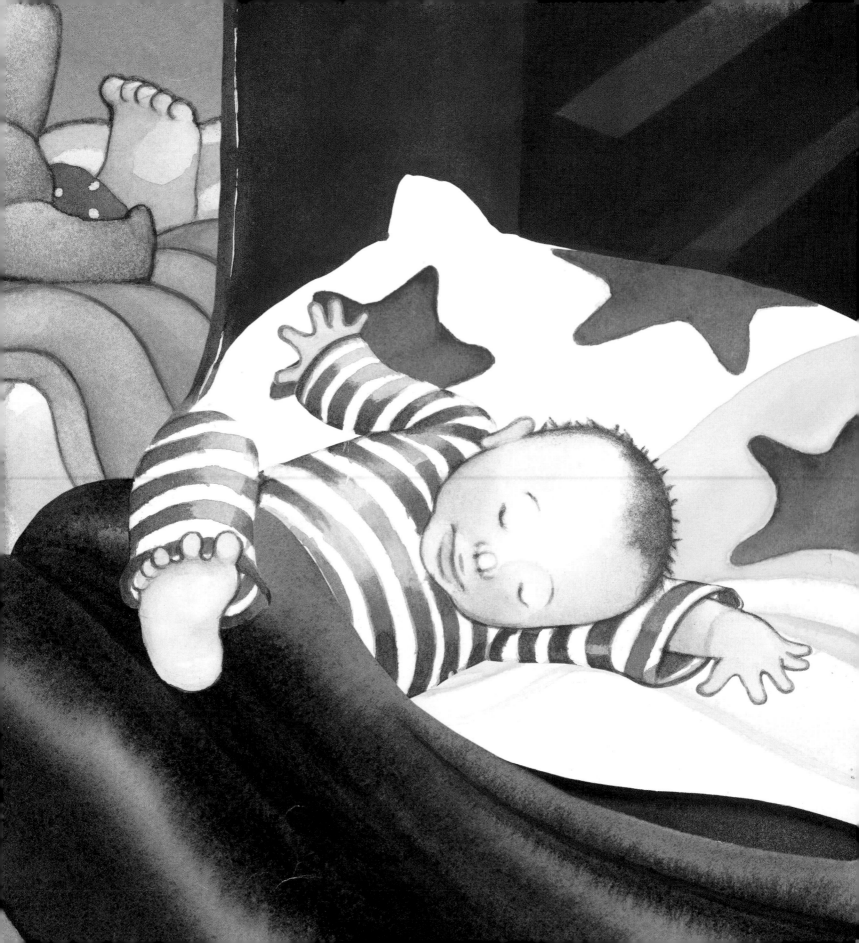

"I'm awake," I say.
"Let's play."

And we jump and we roll
from the bed to
the floor.

You crawl down the hall
to their door. SNORE.

"Let's visit the
monsters' cave,"
I say.

And we creep past

the heap on the chair
to the lair, where it's dark.

There are things that are hairy
and scary that we bump.

And we tumble
and tickle and
scramble and
end up all
tangled, all mingled
and mangled.

And the monsters
rise up ...

and they seize us with grumbling.
And down on the pillows
we're rolling
and tumbling
and giggling
and snuggling . . .

and cuddling and

cuddling and cuddling.